ALL OF YOU Knew

M M KUSHI

To those who escaped, those

still fighting, and

those that we lost..

Chapter One

T he tempered glass shattered, exploding outwards, and I watched thousands of pieces glitter in the sunlight as they fell and skidded across the kitchen floor. It all seemed to happen in slow motion for a few seconds; the glass spraying across the light wooden floors, the chair tipping over and slamming into the ground, the vase of fresh flowers crashing through the center of the table and coming apart on the floor as flower petals joined the ocean of glass. Rage burned brightly in his eyes as he glared at me across the destruction, his knuckles dripping blood onto the floor that had just been mopped.

He stepped toward me and I stepped back, beginning the dance we'd done a thousand times in every room of the house. I tiptoed around glass shards the way I tiptoed around my marriage, afraid to get cut. He surged forward, unafraid of the sharp pieces that so easily sliced my skin and bruised my heart. He smiled at me, the kind of smile the lion gives to the lamb before slaughter... the kind that didn't reach his eyes.

"James," I begged, hoping the shake in my voice would quell some of the rage. "James, please." I lifted my hand, holding it between us, an offering of peace in a war I never agreed to fight. "Please don't do this."

"How many times have I told you, Harbor?" he ground out. "How many?" His fist slammed into the wall and bits of gray paint fell like snow.

I jumped and stumbled back, my careful planning to avoid the glass failing as my bare foot came down on a shard that cut deep into my heel and left a puddle of blood under me. "James," I cried, tears burning my cheeks. "Please stop."

He only advanced on me, glass crunching under his heavy steps. "I asked you to do one thing, Harbor." His words were measured, careful. He was always careful. "And you couldn't even manage to do it *right*." I wilted under the intensity of his anger, crumbling as I had done a hundred times before. There was no stopping him now.

"I'm sorry," I whispered, bowing my head.

"Sorry?" he hissed. "Sorry doesn't fix it."

Stars erupted in front of me, my cheek catching fire as the crack echoed in the otherwise empty room. I stumbled, more glass embedding itself in my feet as my arms pinwheeled at my sides, searching for the wall to try and save myself. My fingers brushed the cool surface but I was too far to stop it and I collapsed onto the floor, dozens of shards driving themselves into the tender skin on my back.

He loomed over me, hatred rolling off of him in great waves that crashed over me and threatened to drown me. Maybe one day he'd finish it and let me be free of him.

I was strong once... wild. My parents called me a challenge, a difficult child that made their lives a living hell.

Mother always told me I'd pay for what I did... I wish I hadn't shrugged it off.

...I should have been a better child.

Chapter Two

I regarded the girl in the mirror with the same quiet hatred that my husband did. Bruises blossomed like flowers across her skin, brilliant hues of purple and red blotting out the sickening shades of green and yellow. Her lip was split down the center, the skin torn open and raw, droplets of blood smeared across her chin and cheek.

How could she let this happen to her?

I lifted the makeup sponge and dotted it along the largest of the bruises, blending his sins away, hiding the monster that I knew he was from the rest of the world. One by one they vanished, carefully painted over with layers of makeup until the face looking back at me almost resembled the girl it belonged to. I took a deep breath and touched the glass, letting my fingers drift over the cool surface. I touched the reflection—far more tenderly than James had ever touched her—and sighed.

Maybe one day she'd be free.

"Harbor?" His voice had lost the razored edge, but I still tensed at the sound of my name on his lips. "Harbor, I'm sorry."

I swallowed and turned, forcing a carefully practiced smile onto my face. "It's alright," I lied. "I'm alright."

He nodded and adjusted the button on his wrist before smoothing down the front of his white collared shirt. "Are you ready to go?"

"Almost," I answered, still smiling. It was better to smile... better to lie.

He nodded. "Please hurry." The common pleasantry sounded alien on his lips. Rarely did he ask me please, and even more rarely did he mean it.

"Of course."

He turned and walked back into the hall, the air around me still humming with the electricity of his presence. I closed my eyes for a moment before standing and making my way over to the bed where I'd laid out the dress for tonight's party. The pale blue fabric was selected to compliment his tie and I ran my fingers across it, admiring the softness. I sighed and exchanged my sweatpants and sweater for the dress, the neckline cut just high enough to hide the secrets written on my chest, the sleeves just long enough to cover the ones on my arms. I turned back to the mirror and frowned, tucking a stray hair back into the bun I'd arranged it all into and adjusting the hem of the skirt.

One day I'd be free.

I pushed my tongue against the back of my teeth as I stared at the painting on the wall. It was all harsh lines and explosions of color. Emotions poured out onto a canvas.

James would hate it.

My gaze slid back to the crowd of people, the dull roar of their voices settling around me. They moved slowly between the tables covered in white satin cloths and decorated with vases overflowing with pale blue roses that matched the color of my dress perfectly. My eyes settled on James, his dark hair and handsome face the perfect disguise for the predator that lurked just beneath the surface. His attention was taken by the beautiful blonde flashing a bright smile as she twirled, the skirt of her deep red dress flying out around her. James hated the color red. Her honey eyes sparkled when she looked at James and I frowned. Would she still smile at him like that if she knew the truth? If she saw the monster?

"Enjoying being a wallflower?" a deep voice rumbled from beside me.

I jumped and glanced over, finding a tall man with a warm smile and eyes that twinkled like the chandelier above our heads. "Oh," I stuttered, my face turning red. "I'm just not one for crowds."

He nodded and raised his hand, waving one of the waitstaff over. "Wine?" he asked as they made their way to us.

"No, thank you." Drunk Harbor did things that sober Harbor paid dearly for... like think she could escape.

"No?" he asked, raising a brow.

I shook my head. "I'm sorry." The response was so practiced and fell from my lips without a thought.

He paused. "Why are you sorry my dear?"

More heat rushed to my face and I ducked my head slightly, looking back out at the crowd of people, finding James staring at me. My stomach dropped and my heart leaped into my throat. I would pay for this moment. "I'm afraid I have to go," I murmured, stepping away from him, inching toward James and the blonde still beaming at him.

"I didn't even catch your name," he protested.

"I'm sorry," I said again, taking another step. He frowned and I turned away, hurrying to James, weaving through the tightly packed bodies and tables. The closer I got, the deeper his frown became until he was scowling at me. I slowed, fear taking root in my stomach, my heart hammering in my chest and echoing in my head. Tears dammed behind my lashes and I blinked rapidly, trying to stop them before they ran down my cheeks. I forced a soft smile onto my face and took another step toward him, hoping he would at least play along for the crowd. "This party is lovely, isn't it?" I asked gently, stopping just in front of James and looking up at him through my lashes.

"Making friends?" he asked, the edge in his voice telling me my interaction with the strange man wouldn't be forgotten anytime soon.

"No."

He was faster than I was prepared for, his hand snaking around my wrist and squeezing until I felt my bones shift in his grip. I bit the inside of my cheek to avoid crying out and he pulled me close to him, our chests only inches apart. He inclined his head and whispered to me. "Don't fucking lie to me Harbor."

"I—I'm not," I stuttered.

He squeezed harder and it became increasingly difficult to avoid screaming. Sometimes I wondered what would happen if I screamed.

Would they help me?

"Harbor," he hissed. "Stop acting like a whore."

Heat rushed to my face, burning up my neck and across my chest. "I'm sorry," I relented, hoping he'd let me go.

He scanned the curious onlookers nearby and smiled politely at them before planting a soft kiss on the same cheek he'd bruised hours before. "We'll talk about this when we get home."

Maybe he'd kill me this time.

Finally, he released my wrist and I quickly covered the injury with my other hand. "I just have to run to the restroom," I said softly, turning from James and walking swiftly in the direction I'd remembered seeing a bathroom sign.

The small room was scented with lavender and tiled in bright white accented by shades of deep purple and flashes of silver. I stood in front of the large mirror, staring into a stranger's face, her eyes red from fighting the tears, her lipstick fading in the center and threatening to expose the cut splitting the bottom one in half. I set my purse on the counter and pulled the tube out, carefully reapplying, protecting her abuser yet again.

One day she'd be free.

"Miss, are you alright?" I jumped and spun toward the door, the lipstick still clutched tightly in my hands. The woman smiled softly at me, her youthful face framed by short curly dark hair that accented her tawny skin that appeared to be lit with gold from within. Her large dark eyes met mine and she frowned. "Miss," she repeated, "are you alright?"

I nodded and fumbled to put the cap back on the lipstick. "Yes," I said quickly.

"Are you sure?" Concern laced through her voice and I paused, my hands shaking.

What would happen if I told her the truth? If I finally told someone about the monster I married?

"I'm sure," I lied.

She nodded, but regarded me like she knew my secrets. I reached up to touch the collar of the dress, making sure the neckline hadn't slipped and revealed the large bruise in the center of my chest. I offered her a smile and finished checking my reflection in the mirror, ensuring there was no evidence of my suffering on display for everyone to see. How embarrassing to let them know that I was weak and breakable... a punching bag for the man who stood at the front of a church and promised to love me forever.

If only he hadn't been lying...

Chapter Three

The scent of alcohol clung to James and filled the backseat of the car. The leather seats creaked under him as he adjusted, trying to get comfortable. "Why do you always do that?" he slurred.

"Do what?" I whispered.

"Embarrass me?" Even drunk, the edge was there, sloppily sharpened and aimed in my direction.

"I'm sorry," I repeated, the chant almost as familiar as my heartbeat.

"Sorry doesn't fix shit, Harbor," he growled.

The driver shifted uncomfortably in his seat, his eyes watching James through the rearview mirror. He was new, still not used to James and me... still unaware he was expected to look the other way.

"James, please," I pleaded. "I didn't mean it."

My teeth clicked together, the cut in my lip reopening as I yelped and covered my face with my hand. James would be furious if I got blood all over the light-colored interior.

"Why are you so useless?" he demanded.

I stifled my sobs. "I don't know," I cried. "I—I'll fix it, I promise."

James shook beside me, rage rolling off of him in huge waves that filled the space in the car. It became all I could feel, and I choked on it with each breath. It took root in my lungs, spreading through the rest of me and stealing all the joy and all the warmth... leaving a familiar, cold emptiness behind.

His hand was rough against my skin as he held my chin and forced me to look into his face. "My mother was right about you," he hissed. "You're just a worthless whore from a filthy bloodline. I *never* should have agreed to marry you." He squeezed my face until I yelped and then shoved me away from him. I slammed into the car door with a thump and remained there, curled into a ball on the seat, still trying to cover my face and keep the blood from ruining the car. The driver's eyes were reflected in the mirror. He stared at me, pain hidden in the depths, his lips drawn into a hard thin line that remained closed, despite the stars that danced in front of my eyes again and again as James worked his anger in the only way he knew how.

Silk sheets were always soft against bruised skin, the cool fabric slipping across a battered body lightly enough it didn't sting and jostle the fresh injuries. I stood at the foot of the bed, wrapped in my bathrobe, staring at the blood stains sprayed across the cream-colored sheets.

Another set for the trash.

The door creaked open and I turned my face, hiding my weakness from the intruder.

"I'm here for the sheets," the soft voice announced.

I nodded and retreated to the bathroom, closing the door and resting my back against it. The mirror beckoned to me but I refused to move, afraid to see the woman looking back at me... afraid of what her face looked like this morning.

The warmth of my blood startled me as it ran down my legs and pooled on the tile floor, forming an ocean at my feet. I stared at it for a few seconds, wondering how long it would take me to bleed to death.

Too long.

I touched the tender skin, my fingers coming back stained scarlet. I rubbed them together and sighed. Every move I made seemed to make me bleed these days, old wounds tearing open with every step, an outline of every blow he dealt me.

I walked to the shower and turned it on, listening to the water smash into the glass, and watching the droplets race toward the floor. Steam filled the spacious room and I let my robe fall to the floor, keeping my eyes fixed on the tile. I could feel the bruises—I knew they were there. Everything ached, my body a map of his rage and destruction. He was a wrecking ball and I was nothing more than a glass house... fragile and breakable.

The water stung when I stepped under the spray, my skin turning pink as heat was forced into it. I dipped my head into the hot spray, cleansing the stench of sweat and alcohol from the strawberry blonde strands. If I closed my eyes, I could still smell him... could still feel him. My chest ached almost as much as my thighs and I finally risked a look down, my stomach turning at the horrors I found.

Large purple splotches adorned my legs like paint stains and blood still ran in a little pink river toward the drain in the center of the floor. Tears streamed down my face, mixing with the water and vanishing just as my screams had done the night before.

No one ever heard the screams.

The water had gone cold at least twenty minutes ago but I remained under the spray, hoping eventually, it would wash away all of the pain and the suffering. I jumped and bit down on a yelp when someone knocked on the door and the same soft voice from before called into the bathroom.

"Mrs. Montgomery, there is someone downstairs to see you. A Mrs. Hart."

My blood turned to ice in my veins. "Thank you," I chimed, trying to force the sound of joy into my voice. "Please tell her I'll be right down."

"Of course, Mrs. Montgomery."

The door clicked closed and I turned the water off, standing in the center of the shower, trying to find the strength to go downstairs and face her. I opened the glass door and grabbed the white towel from the counter, wrapping myself and hurrying back into the bedroom.

The bed was remade, a fresh comforter laid down with the pillows arranged carefully against the headboard, and a simple pair of black leggings and a blue sweater laid out for me. I slid into them and returned the towel to the bathroom, dropping it into the hamper and sweeping my hair up into a clip.

My mother was waiting impatiently in the living room, scanning the space and searching for anything not up to her standards.

"Hello, Mother," I said, forcing a smile onto my face.

She beamed when she looked at me, an expression that quickly soured when she studied my face. "Harbor dear," she scolded. "You really *must* remember to put on some makeup." She shook her head. "What would James say if he came home and found you like that?"

"Nothing," I answered with a sigh. "Is there something you want, Mother?"

She *tsked* at me and frowned harder. "Why would I want anything Harbor? Can't a mother just stop by to see her daughter?"

I crossed my arms. "You never stop by to see me unless you want something." There was a soft defiance in my words, one that I never used with James but was unafraid of with her. She could never do worse than what James already did.

Her perfectly lined lips pursed. "Your father wanted me to invite you and James to dinner tonight. Beatrice will be there as well."

"No thank you," I answered.

She laughed, an emotionless sound. "Dear," she chirped, "it wasn't a question. I am telling you, you and James are coming to dinner tonight. Your father has business to discuss with James and Beatrice and I want to see you."

Even my own mother still bullied me.

"Fine," I answered tightly. "What time?"

She clapped her hands together. "Excellent. Be there at five. Make sure you look nice, I want to take some photos." She stood up and brushed off her skirt. "Do make sure you put on some makeup, Harbor. Those bruises are ugly."

"Of course, Mother," I mumbled.

13

"Don't mumble," she scolded. "How many times have I told you not to mumble?"

"Sorry," I replied, careful to avoid angering her further. "We will see you at five."

She smiled. "See you at five, sweetheart."

She brushed past me as she headed for the door, her presence not nearly as suffocating as James's but close enough to leave me breathless and shaking. I glanced up at the clock. Only five more hours until James was due home. Hopefully, my mother had stopped at his office before coming here. I detested telling James of my mother's dinner plans—they always ended up being my fault.

"Mrs. Montgomery?" the soft voice questioned from the space between the living and dining room. "Are you alright?"

I looked at her and nodded. "I am, thank you." Her face was skeptical, I could see it in the creases on her forehead and the pinched skin at the corners of her eyes. "Really Joy," I insisted, "I'm alright." She stared at me for another moment before nodding and turning away, vanishing into the dining room to continue her duties around the house.

New staff were always troublesome. They always wanted to help. Always thought that they could save me from James and the life I'd been born to live. They gave me hope and made me brave... two things that always ended with me bleeding on the floor.

Chapter Four

I stared quietly at the simple red box sitting in the center of my bed, its large white bow glimmering in the dim sunlight streaming through the open window. A simple white tag dangled from it, my name scrawled across it in James's handwriting. He'd gone to that shop downtown, the one that wrapped your gifts for you. I stepped closer to it.

Another apology gift.

A light wind gusted through the window, causing the sheer curtains to billow outward and the droplets of water still clinging to my hair and skin to chill me. I grabbed the tie of my bathrobe and pulled it tighter, as if that would keep out the cold that was slowly settling into my body.

He would expect a thank you when I went downstairs. I lifted the box from the bed, holding it with two hands despite its small size, and staring down at the paper... it was the same color as my blood.

A coincidence, surely.

I flipped the tag over, finding *I'm sorry* written across the other side. I took a deep breath and tugged the bow off, letting it fall to the floor before tearing into the paper. The simple black velvet box looked like all the others he'd given me. I ran my fingers lightly across the top before opening it.

The diamond glittered brightly even in the dull light, the pendant hanging from a thin silver chain that looked as breakable as I was.

He'd expect me to wear it.

He took great pleasure in parading me around in front of people to show off his wealth. I touched the stone softly. It had probably cost him a small fortune.

Too bad it meant nothing.

"You look beautiful," he said, holding his hand out to me as I reached the bottom of the staircase, and smiling. I froze. Was it another trap? "What's wrong?" he asked, confused.

I shook my head and put my hand in his. "Nothing." I swallowed hard. "Thank you."

He looked pointedly at my neck. "Do you like the necklace?"

I nodded. "It's beautiful. Thank you."

He smiled and shifted almost uncomfortably, casting his eyes downward. "I love you," he lied.

The words sounded foreign and I stared at him. He hadn't said he loved me in years.

"I love you too." Another lie.

He nodded. "I'll be better," he promised.

I smiled, letting him lie to both of us.

"You know I hate going to your parents," James ground out in the seat beside me, his knuckles turning white as he gripped the steering wheel.

"I'm sorry," I answered, staring out the windshield.

He sighed. "Stop apologizing Harbor, it's irritating."

"S—" I bit my tongue to stop the word from tumbling off my lips and he glanced at me briefly before returning his attention to the road ahead of us.

"Besides," he continued, still not looking at me, "I'm the one that should be saying sorry."

"It's okay."

"Don't do that."

"Sorry."

"Harbor," he gritted.

I clamped my mouth shut and folded my hands neatly in my lap, hoping to pacify him.

He took a deep breath and blew it out slowly. "I'm sorry for last night." He paused. "And for yesterday afternoon. I know you were fond of that table."

Sometimes it was nice to hear James say he was sorry for hurting me. It felt like validation that I wasn't deserving of his torture.

Too bad he never meant it.

I took a deep breath through my nose as I raised my hand to knock on the large dark wood door. Massive vases overflowing with greenery stood sentry on either side of it, my mom's addition no doubt. My father hated plants almost as much as he hated his children. The door swung open and a pretty woman smiled at us and ushered us in.

"There you are," my mother announced from the doorway to the foyer. "You're late."

"My apologies Mrs. Hart," James lied. "Traffic."

My mother stared at him harshly for a moment before smiling tightly. "Please, call me Denver." The smile fell from her face. "As I've instructed you to do a dozen times dear."

James returned her smile, all teeth and malice. "Denver," he repeated.

She nodded and focused her attention on me. "Harbor," she sang, as though she were happy to see me. "Let me look at you." She came forward. "Simon is in the foyer, James."

James nodded. "Thank you." He maneuvered his way around my mother and vanished into the next room, leaving me alone with her.

"You look much better than you did earlier." She placed a hand on either of my shoulders. "Though I don't understand your insistence to match whatever you wear to his tie," she scoffed. "I've told you that periwinkle is your color and yet you always show up in these washed-out blues." She shook her head. "I suppose I'll have to gift James a periwinkle tie for Christmas and hope he wears it."

"Of course," I replied, forcing a soft, practiced smile.

Her face turned serious. "That woman is in my house, dear."

"Who?" I questioned.

She scowled at me. "Beatrice," she hissed. "Who else but the serpent queen herself?"

"She's not that bad, Mother." She's worse.

Before she could respond, Beatrice appeared in the doorway, her dark hair swept back from her face and arranged in an elaborate bun at the nape of her neck, her deep green dress fitted just right to accentuate her hips and long legs. "Harbor," she cooed, poisoned honey dripping from her voice. "James said you were in here."

Beatrice was a vast, moonless sky compared to my mother's sunshine. One would freeze you while the other burned.

She came further into the room, stopping beside my mother. "I must say," she clicked, "you did manage to produce quite a beauty, Denver." It was the only praise Beatrice ever bestowed on my mother and it killed her. "Too bad she's an idiot."

She could never let her just have the compliment.

Beside her, my mother looked underdressed for her dinner engagement. Beatrice

19

never went anywhere without ensuring she looked impeccable, a trait James seemed to have inherited from her. My mother favored soft pastels and loose, flowy updos in her home while Beatrice loved dark, broody things and carefully manicured styles that looked uncomfortable and sometimes painful.

My mother glared at the side of Beatrice's face. "She gets her beauty from me," she chimed softly. "And her intelligence from her father."

Beatrice snapped her attention to my mother and frowned. "I'm sure she gets both from you, dear." My mother pursed her lips as Beatrice closely examined my face. "You must try harder, Harbor," she sighed, touching the cheek where the largest of the bruises lay hidden under makeup. "Perhaps a more full coverage foundation," she suggested.

"Yes," I murmured, "thank you."

She waved me off. "It's no trouble at all." She frowned. "Though you must stop upsetting him so much," she scolded. "It isn't good for him to get so riled up."

I dropped my head. "Of course," I mumbled.

"Harbor," my mother snapped. "Stop mumbling."

I lifted my head and stared at her. "Sorry."

Beatrice sighed. "I don't know how my son puts up with you sometimes."

She knew exactly how her son *put up* with me.

"Mother?" James asked from the entry to the foyer.

Beatrice smiled brightly as she turned. "Yes?"

"Please stop fawning over Harbor and let her come see her father, he has been asking about her."

No, he hasn't.

Beatrice frowned, her face turning a shade of pink. "Of course," she said quickly, glancing back at me. "Come along Harbor."

Together, she and my mother carted me into the next room where my father was waiting. He never wanted to see me, he was all too happy to spend all evening talking to James. It was James who wanted some kind of distraction in the room, something to draw my father's attention away from him so he could relax and have a few drinks in peace.

"Harbor," my father's voice stirred the fear in my stomach and I forced a smile onto my face.

"Hello," I said softly, glancing at him and moving to stand closer to James. I was a bunny in the fox's den.

He grinned at me the same way James did when I'd done something to displease him. "James tells me you two still haven't had any luck with giving him an heir?" The tone of his voice made me shiver and I lowered my gaze to the floor.

"That's right," I answered.

He clicked his tongue. "You must try harder. James needs children to continue his legacy. Strong, healthy boys, Harbor."

"Yes," I replied. "Of course." I glanced at James. "I will try harder."

Maybe the fault wasn't with me, but the blame would be laid at my feet nonetheless.

My father made a sound of approval in the back of his throat. "That's my girl."

I smiled tightly at him. It was the closest thing to praise I would ever receive from him and it made me sick to my stomach. Even if I managed to produce a child or two, my position in life wouldn't change.

The doors to the dining room opened and the same woman from the door smiled at each of us. "Dinner is ready," she announced.

"It's about time," Beatrice grumbled, heading for the open doors. "I thought you meant us all to starve to death, Denver."

My mother smiled brightly. "That thought never crossed my mind," she chirped. My father rose from his chair, straightening his tie as he did. He looked pointedly at me and I stepped to the side, allowing him to walk past.

"Harbor," James mumbled, holding his arm out for me to take. I took a deep breath and rested my hand on him, smiling brightly the way my mother had done with Beatrice. It was all an act... a production to save face and make the world believe that everything was perfect in paradise. The picture of grace and abundance, spitting insults wrapped up in pretty bows across the dinner table.

Together, my husband and I walked into the dining room, and I flashed my most dazzling smile as James led me to the chair beside my mother and pulled it out, ushering me into it. The table was set with her favorite place settings, everything dripping in pastels and diamonds. Beatrice wrinkled her nose for only a moment—a fleeting crack in the facade.

"What a lovely design," she gushed, grinning at my mother from her spot across the table. "It's very"—she pressed her tongue onto the roof of her mouth—"*you.*"

Unflinching, my mother smiled politely and arranged her napkin on her lap. "Thank you, Beatrice." The venom in her words was a gold thread woven through it, glimmering only if you knew how to pick the rest of it apart.

"I'm starving," my father announced, settling in his chair and scanning the room.

The woman from the door nodded once and dashed from the room, leaving us to stare at one another and pretend we enjoyed the company. It was a relief when the meal was brought in and laid before each of us. It smelled of decadence and wealth, a rich aroma that filled my lungs.

"It looks wonderful, Lila," my mother cooed, grinning at the young woman.

She dipped her head, "My name is Sarah, ma'am."

Chapter Five

You could have heard a pin drop in the silence that settled over the room, an air of discomfort descending with it.

"What?" my mother bit out.

Sarah steeled herself, squaring her shoulders. "My name," she repeated, "is not Lila. It's Sarah."

"Your name?" my mother ground out through clenched teeth, her lips still curled into a tight smile, "I got it wrong?" She rose from her chair and beckoned to Sarah.

It was a trap.

Sarah moved toward her, closing the distance and nodding her head. "It's alr—"

The smack echoed through the room and Sarah's surprised yelp followed almost instantly, her hand flying to cover her wounded cheek.

"Your name means nothing to me," my mother spat. "*You* mean nothing to me." She stood, towering over the smaller woman. "You will answer to whatever I call you. Understood?" Sarah nodded, tears streaming down her face. "Get out of my sight."

Sarah scampered from the room and Beatrice made a disapproving sound in the back of her throat. "Good help is hard to find," she sighed.

The lines in my mother's face smoothed out and she sat back down slowly. "Yes," she replied, "it is." She looked at me. "Where did you find the woman that answered your door this morning?"

I smiled. "James hired her."

"James?" Beatrice asked, looking at her son.

James smiled tightly. "Yes," he answered. "She was recommended by someone at work. They were downsizing on staff after a death in the family."

Beatrice nodded. "Well, that's lovely." She picked her fork up and smiled at all of us.

The upstairs hallway looked the same way it had when I was a child, bright and cheery with paintings decorating every inch of free wall space. The doors were all closed, hiding secrets behind the heavy wood. I grabbed the knob for the bathroom and turned, surprised to find it locked.

I knocked softly. "Hello?" I heard sniffling from within and frowned, knocking again. "Are you alright?"

The door flung open and Sarah stood silhouetted by the white light behind her. "Sorry," she gushed, her face and eyes red, the outline of my mother's hand still on her cheek.

"Are you alright?" I asked again.

Fresh tears rolled down her cheeks and she shook her head sadly. "No," she sobbed.

I reached out, touching her arm lightly and trying my best to smile. "I'm sorry," I whispered.

Sarah shook her head. "It's not your fault."

I sighed. "I know how awful she can be," I mumbled. "I know how cruel and how mean." I stepped closer to her. "I know that she's a monster."

Sarah's tear-filled gaze settled on my face and recognition flashed in her eyes. She stepped back. "Mrs. Montgomery," she gasped. "I'm so sorry." She wiped her face roughly with her hands.

"Hey," I said hurriedly. "It's alright. You don't have to be afraid of me."Fear exploded in her eyes and she sniffled. "I'm Harbor."

"I know who you are," she grumbled. "You're their daughter."

"I am," I confirmed. "But I'm nothing like them." She regarded me with skepticism and I laughed. "I know it's hard to believe that they produced anything other than a carbon copy of themselves." I dug around in my purse and pulled out the little tube of concealer. I held it out to her. "It might not be your color. You get to go out in the sun more than I do. But it will help hide the bruise."

"Why?" she asked.

"Because seeing the mark will just make her mad again."

"How do you know?"

I sighed. "Because she used to hate seeing mine... she *still* hates seeing mine."

"Mr. Montgomery?" she breathed and I nodded. "Surely your parents will take you back if you tell them."

I shook my head. "They won't. I'd be a disgrace to the family name."

She frowned. "Isn't there something they can do? You're their daughter."

I laughed without humor. "Just don't make him mad," I whispered, repeating the words my mother had said to me the first time I told her James was a monster.

Realization dawned in her eyes and she frowned. "I'm sorry," she murmured. She took the tube of concealer. "Thank you."

I nodded and she darted down the hallway, vanishing down the smaller, more narrow staircase at the end. Mother had insisted on keeping the servant stairs as she hated seeing them running up and down the main one, dirtying her pretty white rugs.

I locked myself in the bathroom, taking a few deep breaths and praying that I hadn't done anything to earn James's ire this evening. I replayed every moment in my mind, picking it apart. I walked past the large mirror over the sink, refusing to look in it, to see the stranger on the other side of the glass.

I tiptoed down the steps and snuck back into the foyer, perching on the edge of a chair and patiently waiting for James to finish speaking with my father in hushed tones in the office off the kitchen.

"There you are," my mother sighed, coming into the room, her face flushed. "I've been walking all over looking for you. Where were you?"

"The restroom," I answered, smiling at her.

"Did you see Lila?"

"Sarah," I corrected.

She glared at me. "Did you see her or not."

"No," I lied.

She huffed and crossed her arms, one of the most relaxed postures she tended to take with me. "Harbor," she threatened.

"Mother," I answered.

Before she could say anything further, James returned to the room and smiled at my mother, holding his hand out to me. "It's been a pleasure, Denver," he said politely. "Harbor and I must be getting home though." For the briefest moment, he looked like he did seven long years ago... my salvation, the white knight sent to save me from the castle I'd been locked in... a ticket to happily ever after.

"Of course," my mother said brightly, grinning at James. "Hopefully next time we have dinner you'll tell me I'm going to be a grandmother."

James nodded. "Hopefully." He glanced at me momentarily and then returned his attention to my mother. "It was lovely to see you and Simon again," he said, before ushering me toward the front door.

The night air was chilly against my face and I shivered, my breath puffing out in small white clouds. James's body heat was a stark contrast to the air and I fought the urge to lean into his side the way I might have years ago... before I saw the monster under the mask.

Chapter Six

J ames's soft snores floated around me in the darkness, his heavy arm slung across my back, pinning me to the mattress. I turned my face, dragging it across the satin pillowcase. I rested my head against it and stared at him in the pale starlight shining through the sheer curtains. He looked almost peaceful, approachable even, the harsh lines in his forehead smoothed out, the rage in his eyes shut away. He almost looked safe and I had to fight the urge to reach out and touch him, to know what it was like to feel his softness for once.

The room behind him was unfamiliar, so much different from my own down the hall. It was all dark and sharp edges that made me shudder.

It suited him.

He stirred and my gaze fell back to him, studying him, waiting for him to roll over and let me slip back into the hallway to tiptoe back down the hall to my bedroom. I could almost feel the warmth of my shower.

"What are you thinking about, Harbor?"

His voice startled me. "What?"

He laughed and stretched, removing his arm from my back, freeing me. "What are you thinking about?" he repeated, something he didn't do often.

I studied his face, the harsh lines hadn't yet returned. "Nothing," I mumbled.

He frowned. "Harbor," he sighed, "don't lie to me."

"Sorry," I murmured, wincing the second the word filled the space between us. He arched a brow at me and I offered a smile. "I was going over what I had to do in the morning," I lied.

"Liar," he said, his voice light, almost teasing.

My face reddened. "I was thinking about how different you look when you sleep," I fibbed... not a lie, but not exactly the truth.

"And how do I look when I sleep?" he yawned.

I looked down at the bed and ran my fingers across the soft cotton sheets. "Soft," I whispered.

"Soft?" he scoffed and I nodded. He laughed and rolled over, leaving me alone with my thoughts again. "You can go, Harbor," he mumbled, his voice thick with sleep.

I breathed a sigh of relief and slid out from under the blanket, padding to the door and slipping out into the hallway. The house was silent and dark, shadows looming in the corners of the hall and behind the slightly open doors.

My room was in stark contrast to James's and remained the only door in the hall that was closed, especially when guests came. Hours before people flooded the house, the staff would spend time adding vases of pretty pink flowers and paintings of romantic scenes to James's room, making it look as though the two of us shared the bed each night.

I would rather peel my skin off than lay down beside James every night.

All of the softness I'd seen in James's face the night before had vanished, replaced by his burning hatred and rage that ate me from the inside out and left me feeling hollow.

"Harbor," he snapped, stepping closer to me. "What have I told you about ignoring me?" His hand was rough when it grabbed my chin and forced me to look into his eyes. "Harbor," he growled.

"I'm sorry," I whispered.

He shoved me away from him, and I fell back onto the shelf, trinkets tumbling down and smacking into my shoulders and back. I yelped and scurried away from it, sidestepping to avoid James as I blinked the tears away. He grabbed me again and pulled me close to his face, the anger rolling off of him.

"Why do you have to be such a bitch?" he snarled, shaking me. My head snapped back and my neck screamed in agony, strands of hair falling out of my braid and flying around my face as he continued to shake me. "Why?" he screamed.

I couldn't keep the tears at bay anymore; they flowed down my face and dripped onto my shirt. "James," I sobbed. "Please."

I was always begging... always asking everyone around me to stop hurting me, stop bullying me, stop tormenting me.

I was weak and fragile... something easily broken and rebuilt to be shattered again.

A new sensation bloomed in my chest, a vine that crept and crawled through me, taking root deep inside and wrapping around everything it could reach, tainting it with its poison thorns. I clenched my fists at my sides and a tremor of anger raced through me.

I was done being pushed around. Done begging for something better. Done being James's punching bag.

I snapped, reaching the end of what I could withstand and breaking. The movements didn't feel like my own. I watched hands reach between James and me, shoving, pushing him away. He stared at me, stunned.

"Harbor," he growled, stepping back toward me.

"No," I replied, stepping back.

He advanced on me and I turned, running through the dining room he'd destroyed, the remnants of my table long gone, the hole in the wall patched and repainted.

He followed.

The kitchen was empty, the staff busy taking their lunch or running errands for themselves. I scrambled around the large island in the center, desperate to stay out of his reach. With each second, the rage in his gaze burned brighter. When he caught me, I was going to regret it more than I'd ever regretted anything in my life.

"Harbor," he hissed.

"James," I begged. "Please just leave me alone."

He lunged, moving faster than I could and grabbing my arm as I tried to run again. He squeezed and yanked me back, slamming me into his broad chest and glaring down into my face. "What the fuck is your problem? " he demanded. "I give you everything you could ever want." He shook me. "I married you when my parents begged me not to."

"As if I'm supposed to be grateful to be married to a monster?" I screamed.

I wasn't prepared for the slap, the sound of skin on skin tearing through the air and echoing in my ears along with the ringing. He drew his arm back, ready to strike again and I slammed my hand onto the island, searching for something to defend myself.

I was done running.

The knife protruded from his chest, the handle pressing into mine as my shaking hand still held onto it. His eyes were wide as they stared into my face, his breath coming out in short, sharp gasps.

"Harbor," he whispered. "Harbor, call 9-1-1."

His grip on me loosened and I stepped back, shaking my head. "No," I replied, frowning.

Blood poured onto the marble floor, pooling around our feet and seeping into the wooden base of the island. "Harbor," he begged, "please."

I shook my head again and took another step back. "No," I repeated.

He took a shaking step forward and winced, closing his eyes and gritting his teeth. "I promise to get help, Harbor," he lied. "I swear, I won't hurt you anymore."

"You're a liar," I said flatly.

He shook his head and stared into my face. "No," he gasped, "I promise, Harbor. We can have a happy life."

"My chance at a happy life ended the moment I said 'I do'."

Chapter Seven

His breaths were ragged and soft, less and less air getting to his lungs as the seconds ticked by. Scarlet stained his lips and dripped onto the floor at a steady pace.

"Harbor," he begged, reaching out to me, trying to crawl forward.

I shook my head. "No," I grumbled, sliding further from the blood that was still spreading across the floor.

The knife lay discarded beside him, he'd pulled it out even after I told him not to.

I watched the blood quietly as it consumed the floor the way James had consumed my life. He was a virus, a weed that needed to be pulled from the garden.

"Harbor," he pleaded, "call 9-1-1."

"No, James," I answered, a hint of venom in my words. "You never called 9-1-1 for me. Not when you threw me through the glass door. Not when you broke that plate over my back. Not when you pushed me down the stairs. Not when you knocked one of my teeth out." I took a deep breath. "You never tried to do better. You never tried to *be* better." I sighed and pulled my knees to my chest, resting my chin on them. "If anything, you got worse."

His eyes shone with unshed tears. "I'm sorry, Harbor." He sucked in a deep breath that cut off with a painful-sounding gurgle.

I shook my head and pushed the loose strands back from my face. "Sorry doesn't fix shit, James," I mumbled. "You've never been sorry for hurting me."

A large part of the kitchen floor was covered in blood at this point, the small ocean of it slowly rolling toward me, staining the white marble with sin and pain. I moved away from it, running from the horrible thing I'd done.

His breaths grew more shallow and his eyes slid closed, the blood flow slowing down. "Harbor," he whispered, gasping for breath. I stared at him from my spot across the room, my body on fire from the adrenaline coursing through it. He shuddered and blew out one final breath, his body going still.

What had I done?

"Mrs. Montgomery?" The voice was frantic and accompanied by fast, light footsteps. "Mrs. Montgomery, are you alright?"

I lifted my head from its spot on my arm and looked around groggily, taking in the golden glow of the kitchen before my eyes settled on the large scarlet puddle creeping closer and closer to me, almost touching my bare feet.

"Mrs. Montgomery?"

I recognized the voice and searched my brain, trying to match a name to the sound of the sweet soprano that rang out like a bell through the kitchen.

Joy.

I popped up from my spot on the floor, my hands out in front of me. "Joy," I breathed. "I'm alright."

She looked at me with wide dark eyes that shone with a mixture of fear and confusion. "You aren't hurt?" she asked, setting her arm full of bags down on the counter beside the doorway to the dining room. "There's so much blood. What happened?"

"No," I confirmed. "I'm alright."

She nodded and took a step toward the island, glancing behind it and covering her mouth with her hand. "Is he?" She swallowed. "Is he dead?"

"Yes," I whispered, my voice shaking. "It was an accident."

She looked at me and took a deep breath. "We have to get rid of him," she said urgently, glancing over at the clock. "The chef will be here in an hour to start on dinner."

"What?" I asked, her words jumbling together in my brain.

She sighed and stepped closer to him, craning her neck to examine the scene. "We have to move him," she said again. "And get all this blood cleaned up."

"You're helping me?"

She smiled sadly. "He deserved worse than bleeding out on the floor." She walked to a drawer on the other side of the room and tugged it open, pulling a pair of latex cleaning gloves out. "He deserved to be beat the way he beat you."

My heart skipped a beat, quaking at the thought that someone thought I was deserving of something better. That James was deserving of exactly what he did

37

to me. A smile tugged the corners of my lips up, but I quickly wiped it away. Now wasn't the time to be smiling. Not with my husband dead on the floor and his blood slowly inching toward me.

"What are we supposed to do with him?" I asked, glancing at her.

She grinned. "My mom makes soap. She owns a little shop downtown." She pulled the gloves on and picked the knife up off the floor, walking over to the sink.

"Soap?" I asked, confused.

She nodded. "You need lye to make soap." She rinsed the knife under the hot water and scrubbed the blade with the gloves. "Lye can get rid of a body."

"Really?"

She nodded and opened the cabinet below the sink, pulling the bleach out and slowly pouring it over the knife, drenching it and the sink. "She purchases it in bulk." Once she was satisfied with her cleaning she smiled and pulled the gloves off, grabbing a hand towel and drying the knife, sliding it back into the knife block, and turning her attention to me. "Now we have to get him out of here," she said, staring down at James's body.

I nodded. "The guest bathroom downstairs has a big bathtub in it."

"That'll work," she chimed, walking back over to James and staring down at him. "Asshole," she mumbled, grabbing his legs. "You get his arms."

I nodded and rushed forward, stepping into the now cold blood, cringing as it ran between my toes. His skin was cool under my fingers and I stared down into a face that could have been sleeping if it weren't for the stillness. The wrinkles of anger were gone, the rage ebbed away along with his life.

He would never hurt me again.

He was heavier than I thought he would be and I struggled to lift him even a few inches off the floor.

"Come on Mrs. Montgomery," Joy urged. "We have to hurry. Chef will be here soon."

I struggled harder, lifting with everything I had in me, tendrils of panic racing through my system. My legs shook with the effort it took to shuffle to the bathroom, and wrestle James into the tub, his head smacking into the porcelain side. My lungs burned as I sucked down greedy breath after greedy breath.

"Now we clean the blood," Joy said, turning and walking from the bathroom.

I scurried after her. "What are we cleaning it with?" I asked.

"Ammonia."

"Do we have that?"

She nodded. "I've seen Chef use it to clean the inside of the oven." She looked at me. "Get a sponge and the mop bucket from the closet under the stairs."

I hurried to the closet and pulled it open, the door groaning on its hinges. The small space was dark and smelled strongly of damp and cold. I grabbed the bucket and searched the shelves for a sponge, grabbing one happily and dropping it into the bucket, returning to Joy.

"We have to hurry," she said, pulling a jug from the cabinet beside the oven. She looked at me. "Then we'll burn those clothes and the sponge."

Why was she helping me?

M.M KUSHI

Chapter Eight

The flames licked hungrily at the fabric, consuming it greedily, burning away the blood and the evidence of what I'd done. Joy had gone home some hours ago, promising to return at first light with the lye from her mother's shop. She warned me that some things might be left over, things that I would be responsible for grinding down in the blender and sprinkling into the garden beds along the front of the house.

I didn't know if I could do it.

Even now, in the silence of the night with only the crickets and the crackling of the fire for company, a cold, dark space opened in my chest. James was a monster, that much I was sure of. But he had laid on the floor dying, the life slowly draining from his body, and begged me to help him... and I had sat there and done nothing.

Was I the monster now?

As if on cue, my cheek throbbed and I reached up to touch the still-tender skin where he had struck me for the final time and winced.

I was *not* the monster.

Walking through my house without the fear of James lurking around the corners, without the sound of his voice echoing through the halls brought me a sense of calm that I had never truly known. My heart didn't thunder in my ears as I walked up the steps. My breath didn't hitch in my throat when I rounded the corner in the hallway.

The monster was dead.

The vanity in the corner of the room beckoned to me, its velvet chair calling my name as the lamp beside my bed reflected in the smooth glass of the mirror.

Not yet.

I wasn't ready to look at the newest marks.

I crawled into the bed and pulled the blanket up to my chin, snuggling down into it and blowing out a deep breath. Home suddenly didn't feel like a war zone and I was pleased with the emptiness of the house. Thoughts of James and the blood on the kitchen floor faded away as my eyes grew heavy and I relaxed into the cool satin sheets.

Tomorrow I would wake up and it would all have been just a dream... a mixture of nightmare and fairy tale.

"Mrs. Montgomery." Joy's voice echoed in my head and I wrinkled my nose, rolling over and trying to sink back into the welcoming darkness of sleep. "Mrs. Montgomery." I groaned and covered my head with the blanket, trying to chase reality away. "Mrs. Montgomery." Her voice was much closer this time, and there was an urgency in it.

I peeked out at her. "What is it, Joy?"

She smiled sheepishly at me. "I have the lye downstairs." She fidgeted nervously.

"And?" I prompted.

"And Mr. Montgomery's mother called."

"Already?" I asked, yawning. "It's so early."

"Yes," she mumbled. "She wanted to let you and Mr. Montgomery know that she is coming over for lunch tomorrow."

I shook my head. "That's not going to work."

She frowned. "I don't think you have a choice. She seemed pretty set on coming for lunch."

I sighed. "I'll figure something out. I'll tell her James is out of town on business and won't be back for some time." I sat up a little, pushing the blanket down. "She hates me. She won't want to come visit just to see me."

Joy nodded and turned to walk back to the door. "I think we have to cut him up," she murmured.

"What?"

She glanced back at me. "If we want the lye to work quickly we have to heat it. We can't heat the bathtub so he'll have to go in something smaller." She rubbed her face. "That means we have to make *him* smaller."

My stomach turned. "I don't know if I can do that," I whispered.

She took a step back toward me. "We have to," she urged. "You don't deserve to go to prison for killing that monster." She took a breath and smoothed a few stray pieces of hair back from her face. "We have to get rid of him."

I nodded and pushed the blanket the rest of the way down, turning and letting my legs dangle off the side of the bed, the wood floor cold against my bare feet.

"Wear something else you can burn," she said, stepping back out into the hallway. Her hand lingered on the doorknob for just a moment and she glanced at me with large dark eyes that felt as if they could see into my soul.

Had she done this before?

I wanted to ask her but thought better of it. What kind of question would that be? I sighed, burying my face in my hands as the door clicked closed and I was left alone.

What had I done?

I stood and ventured to the closet, sorting through the clothing to find something else I could burn away along with my guilt.

I swallowed the bile back down as we stood beside the bathtub and stared down at James. His skin was waxy and cold to the touch, the porcelain stained red from the bit of blood that had continued to drain after we'd moved him.

"We should get started," Joy mumbled, stepping closer to the tub and dropping to her knees beside it. "The pot is big enough for decent-sized chunks, but nothing too big."

I nodded. "Alright." My throat was dry and sore as I knelt to help her, adjusting to sit more comfortably as she grabbed his arm.

"Hold this," she said simply.

I took the arm and held it tightly as she began to saw. The sound of the blade cutting through flesh and bone tattooed itself into my memory. My stomach lurched and even more bile burned up my throat. I forced it back down and took a deep breath through my mouth.

Bits of bone fell to the floor, each one covered in muscle that still clung desperately to it. I gagged again, biting down on my tongue.

"Almost done," Joy panted, continuing to saw.

I closed my eyes and made sure I still had a good grip. The release of the arm from the rest of him startled me and my eyes flew open. The weight suddenly felt like more than I could bear and it slipped from my fingers, crashing back into the tub beside him with a sickening thunk.

Maybe I should have just called 9-1-1 when he asked.

Now it was too late.

The dismembering of a body took much longer than Joy said it would and seemed to create a bigger mess for us to deal with than the whole body.

"Now what?" I asked, staring at the gore inside the tub. Pieces of skin decorated the tile behind the tub and I swore I could feel some on my face but I was too afraid to check.

"Now the lye," she said, standing and wiping her hands on her shirt. Streaks of blood trailed the places her fingers touched and my stomach turned again. "I have it set up in the garage since it has the most open space." She smiled softly at me. "I'll get the pot and be right back."

I nodded and sat fully on the floor, the cold tile chilling me through the fabric of my sweatpants. Sweat dripped down my face, mixing with my hair and causing strands to stick to my cheeks.

This was a mistake.

My breath came faster and harder, my chest tightening until I was sure I would suffocate. It was as though my lungs weren't getting enough air, as though all of the oxygen had been sucked from the room. I brushed the hair back from my face and sighed, trying to focus on something... anything.

Red.

My eyes locked on the color staining my fingers, and horror blossomed in my chest.

Blood.

A lump formed in my throat and I gagged, my body heaving. I turned and bile seared my throat and spilled into the tub along with the bits of James.

I'd made a horrible mistake.

I heaved again and the phone in the kitchen rang, the shrill screech pounding into my head. I took a breath and pushed myself up from the floor, stumbling out to the kitchen and looking around, finding it empty. Slowly, I made my way to the phone, grabbing it mid-ring.

"Hello?" I whispered hoarsely.

"Harbor?" Beatrice's voice was laced with confusion and concern. "Harbor, why are you answering the phone?"

"Oh," I stammered. "I was near it when it rang so I figured I'd just answer it."

"Mmhmm." She cleared her throat. "Anyway, I was just calling to remind you that I'll be over for lunch tomorrow afternoon."

My head was still swimming and I shook it, trying to arrange my thoughts into a coherent pattern. "James is out of town," I lied, glancing back at the open bathroom door. "I'm not sure when he'll be back."

She clicked her tongue. "That's fine, I know he's always so busy. I'll still come."

"Why?"

"What do you mean why?" she snapped.

I winced. "Sorry," I murmured.

She sighed. "I need to talk to you Harbor."

"About what?"

"Why do you have so many questions today?" She huffed. "It's annoying."

"Oh," I whispered. "Sorry."

"I'll be there tomorrow at eleven. Make sure you're presentable."

"Of course," I responded.

The click of the phone was deafening and I stood for a few moments, the receiver still in my hand.

"Who was that?" Joy asked from the bathroom door.

"Beatrice," I answered, setting the phone back down and blinking tears away. "She's still coming for lunch tomorrow."

Joy froze and stared at me. "You told her James was gone right?"

I nodded. "She said she needed to talk to me."

Joy sighed. "Alright. Let's get this done and cleaned up. Then we can worry about tomorrow."

Chapter Nine

Streaks of crimson flashed in Joy's hair as she ducked her head back into the house from the garage. Her face was flushed, sweat dripping from the end of her small button nose and chin. "This should be the last one," she panted, lifting the pot into the house. I nodded and wiped my face with the back of my hand, smearing more blood across it. "Then you have to blend what's left in the blender while I dump this last bucket into the hole."

"Okay," I answered, stepping into the bathroom behind her. Raw bits of flesh clung to the tile wall beside flecks of skin and chips of bone. A ring of sickening brown and red adorned the inside of the tub and sat in small, half-dry puddles near the drain. My stomach still soured as Joy lifted a foot and dropped it into the pot with a metallic thunk. I sat on the edge of the tub beside her and lifted a chunk of arm, dropping it in along with the foot as chills raced down my spine.

What was I doing?

The hours felt like they had dragged by, each minute like an eternity as we dissolved James bit by bit in the boiling pot of lye. The scent was enough to choke me and I had escaped into the backyard a few times to gulp down mouthfuls of air and cry.

I wasn't cut out for this.

Joy grunted as she lifted the pot, struggling under its weight. I hurriedly grabbed one of the sides, trying to help her. My sweat and blood-covered fingers slipped against the stainless steel and I gasped, trying to get a better grip on it. Together we managed to haul it to the garage and get it situated over the flame.

Carefully, Joy poured a mixture of water and lye into the pot, heating it until steam rolled out and the surface bubbled. I wrinkled my nose as the smell filled the garage, wrapping around me and sinking into the fabric of my clothes. I watched the lye and water boil as we waited for the last of the evidence to vanish so Joy could pour it into the hole we'd dug in the woods running along the edge of the property. I'd never been more grateful to live in a rural location. The closest neighbor was six miles away and the forest land behind the house spanned hundreds of miles of wilderness that would go unsearched.

"I'll dump the pot while you start cleaning the bathroom," Joy said, poking at the mixture with a spoon and frowning.

"Okay."

"Make sure you get everywhere."

The scent of ammonia filled my lungs and I choked on it as I scrubbed the tub, trying to ensure I washed away all evidence that James had ever been in it.

"Harbor?" My mother's voice sent chills through me and I shot up, dropping the sponge and peering out of the bathroom into the kitchen. "Harbor?" Her voice sounded closer and I could hear the tap of her heels on the floor as she looked for me. "Harbor?"

"Yes, mother?" I called back, my voice shaking.

"Where are you?" she demanded. "No one came to the door when I rang the bell so I let myself in."

I cringed. "The bathroom," I answered. "I'm not feeling very well."

"Why does it smell so bad in here?"

Tendrils of panic wrapped around my brain and started to squeeze. "I'm having Joy deep clean everything." I blew out a shaky breath. "Beatrice is coming for lunch tomorrow."

"I don't like that woman," my mother huffed.

"I know, Mother."

The sound of her footsteps grew even closer. "What bathroom are you in?"

"The kitchen."

"Why are you in there?"

I sighed. "I was talking to Joy when I started feeling sick. This was the closest bathroom." I tugged the door shut and leaned against it as she entered the kitchen.

"I need to talk to you, Harbor." Her voice was slightly muffled through the wood.

"About what?"

She scoffed. "Come out of the bathroom."

"I'm sick," I protested, turning the lock on the knob.

"Then I'll just wait until you're done."

"Mother please, can we do this another time?" Ammonia filled the room and my lungs burned as I inhaled it.

"No, it's important."

"Then just tell me," I pleaded.

The sound of her footsteps grew very close to the door and the knob jiggled. "Harbor, why is the door locked?" She jiggled it again. "Open it."

My head swam from lack of oxygen. "No."

"Harbor," she scolded.

"Mother, please," I begged. "Another time. I *really* don't feel well."

"You're being selfish, Harbor."

Selfish always seemed her go-to when she didn't have a real reason to be upset with me. Everything I did was selfish. Everything a sleight against her.

"Please." My chest ached as I tried to limit my breaths, choking on the ammonia.

She huffed. "Fine," she hissed, stomping across the kitchen floor and back toward the entryway. I blew out a sigh of relief and waited until I heard the front door slam shut with more force than she would usually use.

I sagged against the bathroom door and turned the knob, sighing as the lock clicked open and the door swung out. Fresh air rushed into the small space and filled my starving lungs and swimming head. I gagged until I vomited, the sour liquid splashing all over the floor and my clothes.

"Are you alright?" Joy asked, coming back into the house, her hands and hair caked with dirt, a small Ziploc bag with bits of white in it clutched in her hands.

I nodded, still panting. "I will be."

She smiled tightly. "I'm going to take these clothes off and shower. You do the same when you're done and then we'll burn everything in the fire pit." She laughed. "Maybe we'll roast marshmallows while we're at it."

"I don't like marshmallows."

She shrugged. "More for me." She looked down at the bag in her hands and paused. "This is for your garden. Throw it in the blender and then sprinkle it in the soil. It's good for the flowers."

I nodded. "Alright."

I continued to scrub the bathroom as she vanished and tried to think back on my memories of her. She had always been quiet, always watching from the sidelines. She rarely spoke and I had only ever heard her voice for brief periods.

So why was she helping me?

Chapter Ten

"**S**he's going to know I'm lying," I fretted, twisting my hair into a bun and frowning into the mirror.

Joy sighed and frowned. "No, she won't."

I bite my lip softly. "I'm a terrible liar," I argued, adjusting the shorter pieces that framed my face until they were lying just so.

Joy's reflection rolled her eyes. "You've been lying since you got married."

I dropped my hands to my lap and picked at the skirt of my simple gray dress. "This is different," I mumbled.

"Mrs. Montgomery," she huffed. "Everything will be fine."

I took a breath and nodded. "I hope you're right."

She bowed her head and stepped out into the hallway. "I'll go downstairs and wait by the door for her to arrive." She looked at me one last time, her forehead wrinkled deeply. "Try to calm down."

I nodded as she hurried down the hall, her footsteps much slower than my pounding heart. It slammed into my rib cage so hard it was bruising me from the inside out. I looked back into the glass, staring at the reflection of the woman who had built her entire life around a pretty lie.

Joy was right.

I'd been lying my entire marriage. Lying about being happy. Lying about James getting better. Lying about the things that James did to me. I painted my face with makeup, hiding the awful things he did to me.

Why?

Shame?

Was it his or mine?

I turned away from the mirror and stood up, pacing at the foot of my bed.

She'd look for him eventually though. I couldn't tell her that her son was away on business for the rest of her life. Eventually, she would realize that something was wrong.

I sighed and bit the inside of my lip, trying to come up with a plan when Joy appeared in the doorway and smiled tightly at me.

"Mrs. Montgomery is waiting for you downstairs."

I felt the color drain from my face and nodded at her. "I'm coming."

She dipped her head and vanished back into the hallway, the sound of her footsteps fading until I could no longer hear them. I took a deep breath and walked to the door, stepping into the hallway and contemplating if anyone would notice me climbing out one of the windows to escape.

...They probably would.

"I don't know why you keep that girl on your staff," Beatrice huffed, glaring at Joy over the top of her glass of iced tea.

"I'm sorry you don't like her," I answered.

She arched a brow. "She's incompetent," she complained, setting her glass down on the table. "I asked for seven cubes of ice and she gave me nine."

"Beatrice," I sighed, "it's two pieces of ice."

My arm burned where she swatted me, the skin turning red from the force of the impact. "I won't be talked down to by some dirty Hart whore," she snapped.

"Sorry," I murmured, setting my glass down and folding my hands in my lap.

"So," she continued, "are you pregnant yet?"

I shook my head. "Not yet."

She frowned deeply. "I didn't want to have to do this," she sighed, shaking her head. "But you've left me no choice." She took another sip of tea. "If you can't manage to become pregnant by the end of the year, I will have to encourage James to consider divorce."

Divorce?

Guilt exploded in my stomach and I frowned.

Would he really have divorced me?

Did I let him die for no reason?

"I know you don't think he'd do it," she explained. "But the Montgomery family needs an heir. And if you can't do that, then we have to find someone who will."

My guilt was eating me alive. "I understand," I answered blankly.

She smiled. "Wonderful." She took another sip of tea. "Besides, I'm sure it won't be too much of a hindrance for you and your gold-digging mother."

"What?" I asked, an edge in my voice.

She laughed softly. "I'm not stupid, little girl. You Hart women are gold diggers." She shrugged "Your mother flitted from man to man until she landed on your father. She's been sucking him dry ever since." She stared pointedly at me. "And I'm sure you've been doing the same to my son."

I had to fight to keep my mouth from dropping open as rage pooled in my stomach and began to boil.

How *dare* she.

I paid dearly for my status in life.

I scowled at her. "Excuse me?" I seethed. She returned my glare and swatted at me again, shifting slightly on the couch to land a firm smack on my cheek, causing my teeth to click together. We sat in stunned silence for a moment before I pointed to the door. "Get out," I demanded.

"No," she snapped. "This isn't your house. It's my son's."

"He's not here," I growled. "Now get out."

"No." She met my gaze confidently, a smug smirk tugging her lips up.

My hands shook with my anger and I gripped the fabric of my skirt tightly in my fingers, knotting it in my clenched fists. She raised her hand to hit me again and suddenly it was her son sitting beside me, his massive frame towering over mine as he screamed at me for something I'd done to upset him. Panic flooded through me and I reached blindly, grabbing the glass pitcher filled with deep caramel-colored tea, and swung.

The glass exploded around us, the overly sweetened liquid drenching the white couch, Beatrice, and me.

Beatrice sagged forward, blood flowing out of a small cut above her eye, and then fell, crashing into the table. I sucked in a startled breath and the severed handle of the pitcher fell from my hands, coming apart on the floor on impact.

Joy's hands were cool when they touched my face, wiping the tears from my cheeks and whispering words I couldn't quite comprehend. I stared at Beatrice, her body lying on the wooden floor, blood dripping slowly onto it until it formed a small puddle beside her face.

What had I done?

Everything seemed to move in slow motion for a second and I took a shaking breath, staring into the endless darkness of Joy's gaze, faintly aware of the scream echoing through the house.

Someone should stop her.

"Mrs. Montgomery." She shook me firmly.

The screaming continued.

"Mrs. Montgomery." She shook me slightly harder.

I covered my mouth with my hand and the screaming stopped, the silence replacing it and weighing more heavily on me than it ever had before.

"I didn't mean it," I whispered, looking at Joy with wide eyes.

"I know," she answered. "But it's done."

I shook my head. "She's not dead," I breathed, a new panic blooming in me.

Joy shook her head.

"I can't let her tell anyone," I panted, my chest tightening.

Joy stared at me—waiting—as if she already knew what my answer would be.

"I have to kill her."

Chapter Eleven

"**A**re you sure about this?" Joy asked, glancing at me.

I nodded. "I don't have a choice," I whispered. "I can't let her leave."

Joy nodded and stepped back from Beatrice's body. "How are you going to do it?"

Tears stung my eyes. "I don't know," I admitted. I watched the rhythmic way Beatrice's chest rose and fell as she breathed deeply, lost in the throes of unconsciousness. "I should do it before she wakes up though," I mumbled. "That way she doesn't suffer."

"Why?" Joy asked.

A pang of confusion echoed through me. "What do you mean why?" I looked at her. "She doesn't deserve to suffer."

Joy sighed, her face softening. "She tormented you just like Mr. Montgomery did. She hit you and called you names. She was *just* like her son." She dropped her gaze, scowling at Beatrice. "She deserves to suffer."

The coldness in her voice made me shudder and I looked back at Beatrice. I had liked her once, thinking that she was excited for me to be marrying her son... but that turned out to be a lie. She had lured me into a trap just like he did and I fell for it.

Stupid, stupid girl.

"It can't be messy," I murmured. "I can't bear to use that ammonia again." I wrinkled my nose. "I can still feel the burn in my chest every time I take a deep breath."

"What if we freeze her?" Joy offered.

"Freeze?" I questioned.

She bobbed her head and brushed a stray blonde hair back from her face. "If we freeze her, then there won't be any blood to deal with until she thaws."

"How are we supposed to fit her in the freezer?"

She frowned. "Well, we can't use the lye again."

"Why not?" I wondered. "Can't we just put her in a hole and pour it on her? It'll still dissolve right?"

She nodded. "I suppose. It'll take longer though."

I shrugged. "If we take her far enough out into the forest, it won't matter, no one will find her. Then when it's time, we just go back and bury what's left."

"It could work," she mumbled.

"It's going to have to work," I sighed.

"You should kill her out in the woods too. That way there's no cleanup."

I nodded. "That's probably for the best."

Leaves and sticks crunched under our feet as we made our way through the trees, Beatrice's weight balanced unevenly between the two of us with me taking the brunt of it. She sagged in my arms, her breathing still even and deep.

I must have hit her pretty hard.

It didn't feel that hard when I did it.

"How much further?" I asked.

Joy looked around. "Not too much probably. No one wanders around out here except animals anyway."

Joy's concept of not too much felt like a marathon and when she finally stopped, seemingly satisfied with how far we'd gone, I dropped Beatrice, gasping for breath. I doubled over and sucked down as much air as I could, the muscles in my arms and legs quivering from the exertion.

"Are you alright?" she asked, eyeing me.

I nodded and straightened, still panting. "Mmhmm."

She dropped the duffle bag she'd hauled out here with us on the ground and crouched beside it, unzipping it and pulling out two shovels. "Let's get this over with."

"Do you think that's deep enough?" she asked, wiping the sweat from her forehead.

The sun was nearing the horizon and I looked down at the hole and nodded. "It should be."

She nodded and dropped her shovel.

"Why are you helping me?" I asked.

She glanced at me as she stepped closer to Beatrice. "What?"

"Why are you helping me?" I fidgeted with my fingers. "I'm committing crimes... awful ones. And yet you're helping me."

She smiled softly. "I was like you," she replied. "My ex-husband used to beat me all the time. I know what it feels like to be powerless, to wish that your life was different." She rubbed her face with her hands, wiping the sweat away. "No one deserves to feel like that."

"How did you get away?"

"Divorce."

There was that word again...

And the guilt came along with it.

"Oh," I whispered, dropping my gaze to the ground.

"Hey," she said quickly. "He wasn't as bad as Mr. Montgomery." She took a breath. "And if I'm being honest, I wish he was dead. He still has rights to our children and I fear for them every single time they go to see him. I'm afraid he's going to do to them what he did to me." Her eyes clouded with fear and she sighed. "You did the right thing, Mrs. Montgomery."

"Harbor," I mumbled.

"What?"

"My name," I answered, "it's Harbor."

Joy nodded. "Harbor," she mused, as if testing the feeling of my name on her tongue.

"There's no need to call me by his name anymore," I mumbled. "I'm not his anymore."

Joy stepped toward me. "That's right," she said with a smile. "You're free now."

"Almost."

"Almost?"

I nodded. "But that's tomorrow's problem. Let's get this over with." I stepped closer to Beatrice and Joy mimicked me. We each put a hand on her and pushed, rolling her into the hole. She landed with a thunk and a yelp, her eyes flying open and staring up at us from the darkness.

"Harbor?" she groaned. "Harbor what are you doing?"

I peered down at her and smiled tightly. "You don't get to be mean to me anymore."

"My son will look for me," she panted, her eyes wide as she reached out and touched the sides of the hole.

I frowned. "James, won't be looking for anyone."

Dirt fell on her face, and she wiped at it, tears mixing with it and creating streaks of mud across her cheeks. "He loves me," she protested.

"He might have," I replied softly. "But none of that matters now."

Panic took over her features as more dirt fell onto her face and she tried to push it away. "Let me out of here," she begged. "Please, Harbor."

I shook my head slowly. "Why would I do that?" I smiled. "After all, I'm just a gold-digging whore." I kicked a little dirt into the hole and she thrashed, smacking at her face to get it off. "And with you *and* your monster of a son gone, every penny of the Montgomery fortune is mine."

Tears poured down her cheeks. "What did you do to James?" Fear prickled in her voice.

"Nothing that he didn't deserve," I answered. I kicked more dirt into the hole and she stood up, reaching up for the sides. I grabbed one of the discarded shovels and brought it down on her hands, a guttural scream tearing from her lips and echoing in the trees. "I don't think so," I mumbled, watching her. She attempted it again and I smacked her harder. "Do it again and I'll cut them off," I hissed.

Her face reddened. "Harbor," she growled. "That is enough. Let me out."

I shook my head. "You don't get to bully me anymore. You don't get to *hit* me anymore." She reached for the side and I aimed the shovel for her fingers, bringing the sharp end down and lodging it deep into the ground, blood pouring out of the jagged, open wounds and soaking into the earth as she screamed and fell backward, smacking her head off the side of her grave.

Everything was finally silent.

M.M KUSHI

"You don't get to own me anymore."

Chapter Twelve

The blender roared as it crushed what was left of James into a fine white dust. I stared at it as the blades spun, flashing silver in the mini snow-storm. The clock on the far wall ticked loudly in time with my heart and I sighed, hitting the off button. Late afternoon sunlight shone brightly through the open windows, carrying a warm summer breeze with it.

The house felt lighter, the heaviness gone along with James. For the first time, I could take a full breath, my lungs filling with the idea of freedom and happiness.

I gathered the powder from the blender and poured it into a small container, carrying it out to the gardens in the front of the house. The air smelled of flowers and fresh soil as I knelt in the grass and began sprinkling the mixture into the beds.

It would be the only beautiful thing James ever helped create.

I smoothed the soil down, smiling to myself as the sunshine warmed my back and promised me a better life.

"What are you doing?" My mother's shrill voice sent chills waltzing down my spine and I turned, spotting her standing near the front door, her arms crossed. "You're going to ruin your dress."

I sighed. "So?"

She huffed. "Harbor." There was an edge of rage in her words and I quickly finished pouring the powder into the flowers and stood up, brushing the dirt off me and walking over to her, my bare feet sinking pleasantly into the slightly damp grass.

"What is it, Mother?" I asked, stepping onto the porch and opening the door.

"Have you seen Beatrice?"

My blood ran cold. "No, why?"

"Because I can't find her."

"Are you sure she isn't avoiding you again?"

She glared at me, following me into the kitchen. "This isn't a joke, Harbor. What if something happened to her?"

I sighed, set the container on the counter, and walked to the sink to wash my hands. "What would have happened to her?"

She threw her arms up. "I don't know. *Something*." She began to pace. "She always answers me."

"She hates you," I pointed out.

"No she doesn't," she argued.

"Then you hate her."

"I do not," she snapped.

I dried my hands on one of the towels hanging from the oven handle and stared at her. "She called you a whore and a gold-digger... all the time. She called *me* a whore and a gold-digger. She hated you, Mother."

She shook her head. "She wouldn't have let her son marry the daughter of someone she hated."

I rolled my eyes. "It's all about money," I grumbled.

"What?"

"Money," I hissed. "That's all any of you care about." I slammed the towel down on the counter and scowled at her. "You married my father because you wanted his fortune. You trained me to be just like you... to be perfect and pretty and polished... to smile and bat my eyes and let someone abuse me for the sake of having a comfortable life."

She returned my glare with one of her own. "Stop lying, Harbor. James is a good husband. He provides for you, he makes sure you're comfortable. You have a charmed life."

"He beat me!" I screamed, my entire body shaking with rage. "You knew he was a monster. You've always known." I stepped closer to her. "You saw the bruises. You told me to *hide* them."

She shook her head. "He could have done worse."

"*Worse?*" I demanded. "*What* is worse than being tortured and then ignored by the people that are supposed to love you?" I huffed and stared into her face. "But you never loved me, did you?"

She looked offended. "I don't have to stand here and listen to you be a raging bitch, Harbor." She moved to walk back into the entryway and I stepped in her path, blocking her in the kitchen.

"Admit it," I hissed. "Admit that you never actually loved me."

"Of course, I love you, Harbor," she sighed. "You're being ridiculous."

"No," I growled. "You don't stand by and watch someone you love get beaten. You don't let someone you love suffer." I laughed. "You know what, Mother. I tried to love you." I stepped closer to her and she stepped back. "I tried so hard to make myself love you. But with each hit I took from James, that love died. With each bruise I had to cover I started to hate you." She stepped back. "I *hate* you." I stepped forward. "I hate you."

"Stop it," she hissed, trying to step around me.

I grabbed her wrist and she slapped me hard across the face, her nail slicing into my cheek and leaving a stinging sensation behind as my ears rang. I squeezed her arm. "You're no better than James."

"Let go," she demanded, yanking her arm. "*Now.*"

"No." I stepped closer to her, until we were face to face, her erratic breaths washing over me. "I'm not afraid of you anymore, Mother."

Fear erupted in her eyes and she pulled against me harder. "Harbor," she begged, "let go."

I shook my head. "No."

"Harbor," she cried. "I'm sorry, honey. I was wrong. I should have helped you."

"It's too late now, Mother," I whispered. "I've already helped myself."

Her eyes widened. "What did you do?"

"What I had to."

She swallowed. "I can help you." She nodded quickly. "I can make sure you don't get caught."

"I don't need your help."

"What's going on, Harbor?" Joy appeared in the doorway.

My mother's face relaxed a little and she blew out a sigh. "Call the police," she begged, looking at Joy. "Hurry."

Joy looked at me and then back at my mother, shaking her head. "No," she answered, stepping back from the doorway. "I don't think I will." She turned and walked away, leaving my mother and me alone in the kitchen.

"I lied," I admitted. "I do know where Beatrice is." My mother looked at me, her eyes filled with tears. "Would you like to see her?" She shook her head. "Too bad," I mumbled, "because I'm sure she'd love to see you. She's probably pretty lonely out there all alone."

"Harbor," she sobbed, "Please let me go."

"No."

"Your father will be wondering where I am," she objected, stumbling over a large rock hidden among the leaves and tall grass.

Joy snorted and I glared at her before returning my attention to my mother. "No, he won't," I answered. "He has mistresses to keep him busy."

"He loves me," she insisted.

I shook my head. "He doesn't love anything except his money."

Tears streamed down her face. "Harbor," she begged, "please, think about what you're doing."

"I don't have to think about it." I glanced at her. "I know exactly what I'm doing."

"What will you do when James finds out?"

"James isn't going to find out."

"He will," she argued. "I know he will."

I stopped walking and stared into her eyes, frowning. "James is dead."

All the color drained from her face, aging her far past her years as she appeared to resign herself to her fate. "How?" It was barely a whisper and I shrugged as we started walking again.

"It was an accident," I admitted. "I didn't mean it."

"We're almost there," Joy announced, picking up her pace slightly, pushing my mother faster.

Chapter Thirteen

The hole looked smaller than when we'd been digging it, and I crept closer to it slowly. Anxiety made a home in the pit of my stomach and Beatrice's screams replayed in my head, echoing over and over.

"Come say hello," I mumbled, beckoning to my mother.

"No."

Joy pushed her forward and she stumbled, nearly falling head-first into the hole. She put her hands out in front of her, catching herself on the hole's edge, dirt falling into the sludge at the bottom. Bits of Beatrice's face were still visible, small pieces of flesh still clinging to the exposed bone as the lye ate away at her. The dark strands of her hair were gone, washed away and sinking into the earth.

"Look, Mother," I encouraged. "You're finally better than Beatrice." My mother heaved, throwing up bile into the mud and curling in on herself, shoving back from the hole.

"Harbor," she sobbed. "Let me go."

I shook my head. "I can't do that, Mother." I stepped toward her. "You get a choice though." I smiled. "Would you rather go into the hole alive or dead?"

"W—what?"

"You get to choose if you're alive when you go in the hole." I sighed and looked back at Beatrice's remains. "I must warn you though, lye burns."

She shook her head. "No, let me go."

"No."

"Harbor," she growled, mustering some of her strength. "Let me go."

"No." I stepped toward her. "Choose."

"No," she hissed.

"You're leaving it to me?" I asked, arching a brow. "Big mistake." I grinned and stood in front of her, herding her backward as tears streamed down her face, mixing with the vomit and dirt.

"Harbor," she begged. "Please."

"Please what?" I spat.

"Stop," she shrieked.

I crouched down in front of her and smiled sadly. "No." I put a hand on each of her shoulders and shoved.

Her eyes were wide as she fell, plummeting into the hole filled with a mixture of lye and Beatrice. She splashed into it, her screams echoing out of the abyss and bouncing off the trees as Joy moved to the edge and began to pour more lye into the hole.

"Goodbye, Mother."

The heat of the day had given way to the cooler night, stars blinking to life overhead as I stood in the center of the long, winding driveway. Golden light burned out of a few windows, shadows moving swiftly in front of them as the staff readied themselves to leave for the night.

Within the hour, they would all be gone.

I moved quietly into the bushes along the driveway, plopping down on the cool ground and settling myself in to wait. I picked at the flowers growing on the bushes, pulling the petals loose the way James had done to me, and watching them fall to the ground slowly. The side of my face still throbbed and I reached up to touch it, letting my fingers run across it slowly, soothing some of the hurt and sighing. It would be weeks until they were all gone.

Weeks of having to hide inside my house or paint my face with makeup to hide it.

But after that— after that, I would be free.

I would never have to hide my husband's sins again.

As I sat, my mother's screams joined the chorus of Beatrice's cries and James's pleading. They would be with me forever, always there, ready to pounce whenever I had a moment of quiet.

Was I the monster?

I sighed and glanced back at the house, noting the singular light on the second floor still shining in the darkness. The staff had all gone by now and he would be alone, probably sitting in his office.

I stood up, shaking off the sounds of their deaths and the visions of their blood on my hands. I wiped my fingers on the skirt of my dress and stepped out of the bushes, walking slowly up the driveway.

Only one more monster to go.

Joy had promised to be my alibi. I had been holed up with her the whole week, nursing the latest wounds given to me by my abusive husband, who left for business after I threatened to call the police and had not contacted me since. I found myself repeating the story over and over again in my head, trying to memorize all the details for when the cops came knocking, searching for answers I wasn't going to give them. I would play the part of the grieving wife and daughter, left alone in this world with no one to love and protect her from all the monsters.

The door was unlocked, probably left that way in anticipation of my mother stumbling in later, and I stepped inside, looking around the dark space and then hurrying to the stairs. I tiptoed up to the second floor and followed the light that spilled out of the doorway into the hall, bathing the light wooden floor.

"Denver?" my father called. "Denver is that you?"

His voice sounded frail, less angry than when he spoke to me... less edged with a silent hatred.

"You're home late," he called. "Did you see Harbor?"

He had known she was coming to my house.

"Has she managed to do her job yet?"

I sighed, even outside of my presence he was concerned with whether or not I had managed to give James a child and continue the bloodline that was now snuffed out. I paused outside the door, wrapping my hand around the knob and taking a deep breath.

"Hello, Father," I chimed, opening the door and stepping into the office.

He turned in his chair, squinting at me and frowning. "What are you doing here, Harbor?" He sighed. "You aren't trying to come home again are you?"

I shook my head. "No," I whispered.

He nodded. "Good, because I thought I made it clear that you weren't welcome back here. You have a husband and a house."

"I have a house," I corrected.

"What are you going on about?"

"I have a house," I repeated. "Just a house."

He rolled his eyes. "Have you seen your mother?"

"Yes."

He huffed. "And?" he demanded.

"And what?" I asked.

He smacked his hand against the top of his desk. "My God, Beatrice was right. You are an idiot."

I squared my shoulders and stared into his face. "No, I'm not."

He nodded and stood up. "Yes, you are." He moved to turn off his lamp and blow out the candle wafting the scent of cedarwood through the room. "It's a good thing you got your mother's face, otherwise it would have been difficult to find you a decent husband."

"You didn't find me a decent husband."

Chapter Fourteen

He seemed taken aback. "I always knew you were an ungrateful bitch. Just like your mother."

"Ungrateful?" I demanded. "You think I'm *ungrateful?*"

He sighed. "Go home, Harbor."

I shook my head. "No." I stepped toward him. "Tell me how I'm the ungrateful one."

He glared at me. "I don't have time for this."

I stepped in his way, blocking the door. "I'm sorry," I snapped. "I just don't understand how I'm ungrateful when I have given up every single piece of myself to make you happy." Anger and bravery mixed, creating a cocktail I would have once shied away from. "I married that monster and let him beat me and belittle me every single day for years, all because you told me it was my place... it was what I had been born to do. The *only* thing I'd been born to do."

"Harbor," he grumbled. "Get out."

"No."

He arched a brow. "No?"

"I'm sick of being bossed around." I advanced on him. "I'm sick of being told what to do."

"Harbor," he growled. "Enough. Go home."

"I will," I answered. "After I'm finally free of you."

"What are you talking about?"

I touched the bookshelf beside the door, running my fingers across the smooth, cherry wood surface slowly and sighing. "Only one of us is going to survive tonight."

"What are you going to do?" he laughed. "Kill me?" There was a hint of disbelief and amusement in his voice that made a wave of anger surge through me, filling all the empty space.

"Yes," I answered bluntly.

He paused, staring at me as if he were seeing me for the first time. "And how do you plan to do that?"

"Fire."

"You're going to burn me?" he asked.

"Yes. But that won't be what kills you." He tilted his head and sat back down in his chair, his eyes locked on me.

He was finally interested in me... finally seeing me as a person instead of a chess piece to move around a board at his leisure.

"And what will kill me?"

"Smoke."

"Smoke?"

I nodded. "You fell asleep while working and accidentally knocked over the candle on your desk." I gestured toward the still-burning three-wick candle. "It set the curtains on fire and with all of your pretty old books, the room went up faster than you could escape." I stepped toward him. "It will be a horrible tragedy."

"And your mother?"

"Already gone," I replied.

"Beatrice?"

"Gone."

"James?"

"What do you think?"

He nodded silently. "Alright then."

"Alright?"

He shrugged and settled into his chair. "It seems you've made up your mind. And I'm assuming you're sure you won't be tied to the other three."

Doubt blossomed in my stomach and I hesitated. I was only pretty sure I wouldn't be tied to the others. Joy promised I'd be safe, but how could she know?

I stared at him as a smirk spread across his face. "What's wrong, Harbor?"

I shook my head, trying to clear it. "Nothing."

Everything would be fine.

He nodded, leaning back in his chair and rubbing his gray-streaked beard with his hand, studying me. "So what are you waiting for?"

I sighed and stepped closer to him. "You really aren't afraid?"

He chuckled. "Why would I be afraid when I know you won't do it."

"How do you know that?"

"Because you've always been weak."

Anger flashed to life in the pit of my stomach once again, a small flame nurtured by the knowledge that he thought I was too weak to fight back. Too weak to stand up for myself.

"I'm not weak," I ground out.

"You are," he said simply. "You always have been, just like your mother."

"Stop comparing me to her," I hissed. "I'm nothing like her."

"You are," he insisted. "You are a carbon copy of her."

My fingers touched something cold on the bookshelf and I held onto it. "Take it back," I whispered.

He shook his head. "No."

I moved before I could fully comprehend what I was doing, swinging whatever was in my hand and hurling it at his head. When it made contact, I heard the crack of bone, blood exploding out of a head wound. He groaned and slumped back a little, his head tilting to the side as he reached up to touch the blood dripping down his temple.

"You hit me," he mumbled.

I leaned close to his face, the bloodied weapon still in my hand. "Just like you used to do to me, *Father."*

"What the fuck, Harbor?" His speech was slurred, and the sound of a swear word on his tongue made me stop, confused. He never swore. Not once in my whole childhood. He had told me once that people only swore because they were of low intelligence and couldn't think of a better word to use.

"I wish I could say I was sorry," I whispered, frowning. "But that would be a lie."

I held the metal sculpture above my head and brought it down on him again, smacking him hard enough to knock him unconscious, and watching him slump forward, hitting his head off the corner of the desk.

I stood in the center of the office for a moment, staring at what I'd done, the weapon still clutched tightly in my hands. The flame of the candle flickered brightly, back and forth, pushed this way and that by the slightest shift in the air. I reached out slowly, nudging it closer to the curtains.

They would catch quickly and then all I'd have to do was go home and wait.

Wait for the call that my childhood home had been burned to the ground.

That my father didn't make it out.

That my mother was mysteriously missing.

The flames reached toward the midnight sky, licking at the stars and trying to caress the moon. I watched smoke roll from the upstairs windows, my father's office already completely gone.

It would look like an accident.

A horrible accident.

I turned from the scene, walking back down the driveway and onto the street. The car was parked a bit down the road, so no one driving by would notice it.

The night air was crisp, chilling my skin and causing goosebumps to rise on every exposed inch of flesh. The road was uneven under my feet and I stumbled a few times in the dark, managing to catch my balance before I tumbled onto the asphalt. No cars passed as I walked, leaving me alone on the desolate, winding road.

Chapter Fifteen

The black veil in front of my face caused a slight checkered look to everything and I sighed. I should have opted for a different one. Perhaps one with a finer mesh.

Tears rolled down my cheeks slowly and I reached to dab them away with the tissue crushed in my gloved hands. It came away with bits of black from my mascara and I could almost hear my mother's voice in my head, scolding me for ruining my makeup yet again... especially on tears that weren't real.

I glanced down at the deep auburn casket, watching the way the sun reflected its shades of gold and red as it peaked through the leaves. The crowd was silent, staring straight ahead as the preacher spoke lies about what a wonderful man my father had been, listing all of the things that he had accomplished in his life.

They'd asked if I wanted to say something but I'd declined.

They assumed I was too upset. The broken, devoted daughter who lost both her parents in less than a month. The beaten battered woman who suffered in silence at the hands of her monstrous husband.

Most people figured James and Beatrice left the state, moving yet again to start anew as his father had done when things started falling apart for him.

No one asked about him anymore, they left me alone in my great big house on its rural country road, whispering about me when I dared to wander into town.

for something. Pointing and speaking in hushed tones about what could have happened behind closed doors. About what *I* could have done behind closed doors.

Too bad they'd never know the truth of it all.

I knelt in the grass beside the garden, reaching among the pale pink and blue blossoms to grip a weed. I pulled, tearing it out from the root, bits of soil falling from it and raining down on the deep green leaves of the other plants. I laid it beside the stones separating grass from garden and reached for another one.

It was always best to pull weeds out by the roots, then maybe they wouldn't grow back.

I sighed, I'd pulled the weeds out of my life from the roots, and yet their presence still lingered. Their voices filled my head and their shadows stalked my dreams, leaving me restless.

Was I the monster in their absence?

I paused, staring down at the flowers and drawing a deep breath. If I closed my eyes, sometimes I could still see their faces, their accusing eyes boring into my soul and tormenting me with the knowledge that I was a killer.

The small voice in my head assured me I was the victim... the kicked dog that finally fought back and won. But something much more sinister lurked in my thoughts when I was alone, running from the ghost of James's anger... the phantom of my abuser.

I shook my head and pulled another weed from the garden, crushing the stem between my fingers before laying it with the others.

Freedom tasted bitter and lonely, a thick ash that settled on my tongue.

Joy had left before I'd returned from my parents and had not come back. I thought I spotted her in town once or twice, but she ducked away from me before I could be sure, running from the reality of what we'd done.

I couldn't blame her really, I'd run from me too. I was a killer...

But she was the accomplice.

Just as guilty.

Just as monstrous.

I shook the thought away and pulled the final weed from the bed, gathering the others and standing. I made my way to the back of the property and ventured a few paces into the trees, pausing when I heard the rustling of leaves. I turned in a small circle and found nothing except my own anxieties. I opened my arms, letting the plants fall to the ground before walking back to the gardens to gather flowers for the dining table that would be arriving today.

The rustling came again and I turned back, staring into the darkness created by the trees that loomed overhead. Nothing stirred but my heart leaped into my throat and the hair on the back of my neck stood on end.

If I stared long enough... if I looked hard enough, I could almost see the ocean of blood staining the forest floor, bathing the Earth in my guilt.

I frowned and hurried back to the garden, plopping down onto the soft ground.

I brushed the blossoms with my fingers, admiring their softness as they slipped across my skin, like satin sheets across bruises.

Also by

The Shredder Universe

Survivor

Savior

Stand Alones

Darling Dark and Dear

Made in the USA
Columbia, SC
10 November 2024

45750675R00052